SBN 361 04703 7
Copyright © 1979 Beaverbrook Newspapers Limited
Published September 1979 by Purnell Books, Berkshire House,
Queen Street, Maidenhead, Berkshire
Made and printed in Great Britain by Purnell and Sons Limited,
Paulton (Bristol) and London

Marks and Spencer Limited
Baker Street, London, England
1428/3000

Reprinted July 1980

The 3rd *St Michael* ® book of
RUPERT
Favourites

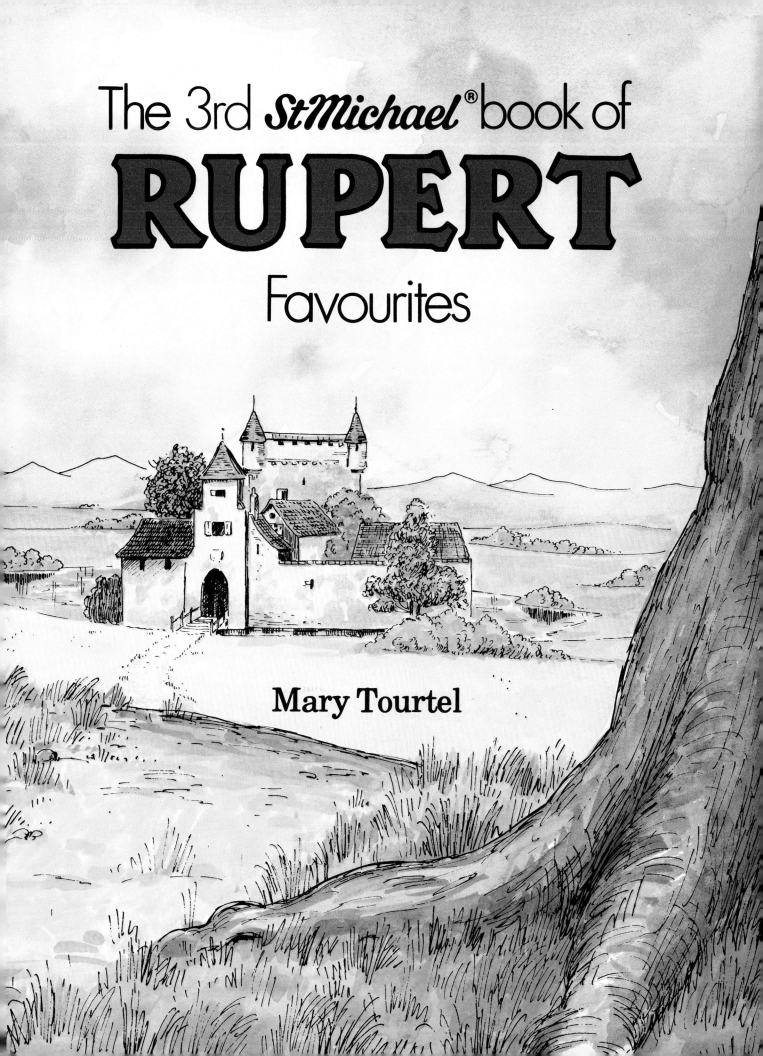

Mary Tourtel

RUPERT

and
Bill's Seaside Holiday

Poor Bill Badger was ill with mumps,
  So Little Bear did find
His way to Mrs. Badger's house
  To ask about his friend.

Said Bill's mother, "He's much better now,
  But you must not see him yet,
Till the doctor says you may.
  Those mumps you, too, might get."

Some days later Mrs. Badger called
  On Mrs. Bear. Said she,
"Bill's better, but the doctor says
  We should take him to the sea.

"So I thought it would be nice, you know,
    If Rupert could come too."
At this Rupert, who was present, cried,
    "Mum, let me go, please do!"

Kind Mummy Bear let Rupert go.
    So next day for the train
They started, for they didn't mean
    To miss it, that was plain.

And on the platform, eagerly,
    There Bill and Rupert waited
With Mrs. Badger; how they hoped
    The train would not be late.

The train came in, they took their seats,
    And glad were both the boys
That the journey would be rather long,
    It added to their joys.

As they drew nearer to the coast,
    They looked out eagerly
From the windows, each one hoped
    To catch the first glimpse of the sea.

Rupert saw it first: "Oh, look!" he cried,
    Where serene and blue it lay,
And very soon, their station reached,
    They arrived at Winkle Bay.

The porter found a taxi for them,
    "Come!" Mrs. Badger cried,
When she'd seen the luggage safe;
    "Come, children, get inside."

Then quickly did they scramble in.
    "Where to?" the driver said.
"To Tinmouth House," Bill's Mum replied;
    "It's on Sea View Parade."

Away they were driven in the cab
    As happy as could be,
And when they came to Tinmouth House
    They found a welcome tea.

Next morning was a glorious day;
    The sun shone warm and bright.
Said Mrs. Badger: "You shall bathe,"
    Much to the boys' delight.

Upon their way who should they meet—
   They could scarcely believe their eyes—
But Mrs. Bunny and the Twins.
   "Well! This is a great surprise!"

Cried she, while Rex and Reggie greeted
   Bill and little Rupert Bear.
How glad they were to see their chums.
   What fun they would have there.

Now, Little Bear could swim quite well—
   His Daddy had taught him
When they'd stayed by the sea before.
   Bill Badger, too, could swim.

"Come on," they said to Reg and Rex,
   "We'll teach you to swim too."
At first the Twins were nervous, but
   They soon learned what to do.

After their bathe they played awhile.
   Until Bill Badger spied
Some donkeys waiting on the sands.
   "Mum, can we have a ride?"

He asked his mother. "Yes," she said.
   They all thought it was grand
When each was mounted on a steed
   And jogging over the sand.

Now when they'd had their donkey rides,
   "What say you to an ice?"
Said Mrs. Bunny. All agreed
   That would be very nice.

So when a café they had reached,
    Kind Mrs. Bunny led
The party to a table there,
    And to the girl she said,

"Six large ice-creams—vanilla, please.
    We'll have a scrumptious feast."
And then they had a plate of cakes,
    And each had two at least.

So did the pleasant morning end,
    And dinner time drew near.
They parted where the Bunnies stayed,
    Said Bill's mother, "Well, my dear,

"We'll meet again this afternoon.
    You will come along with us
To Winklecove. It's rather far,
    So we must take the bus."

The bus for Winklecove stopped
    At the corner of the street
At two o'clock, and on the stroke
    The party there did meet.

The bus came lumbering into sight
    And drew up, then Bill cried:
"Oh, Mummy! Do let's go on top.
    It's nicer than inside."

"All right," she said. Bill led the way.
    "Be careful now. Go slow."
The conductor helped them up the stairs,
    The bus started—off they did go.

When they reached pleasant Winklecove,
    And climbed up to the hill
They sat down there to see the view.
    Mrs. Badger said to Bill:

"Now you can go and play, my dears,
    But don't go far away,
Or near the cliff edge—do take care.
    Meanwhile here we will stay

"And fine and ripe. Let's stop and pick."
  They'd never seen before
Such big ones, and so plentiful,
  All growing there galore.

"And do our knitting; mind you come
  Back in good time for tea,
We're going to have it in that shop
  With the garden near the sea."

Away the four companions strolled.
  They'd not gone very far
When Rex called out: "I say! Just look!
  Wild strawberries? Yes, they are!

The little friends just picked and ate
  From that profusion there,
But the best and ripest they could find
  They set aside with care

For Mrs. Bunny and Bill's Mum.
  "Oh, won't they be surprised
When we bring these along for them
  At tea-time!" Reggie cried.

Said Rex: "Let's have a game of 'Touch',"
   And Rupert was made "He".
They ran and chased about the downs,
   Laughing in their glee.

The nimble-footed Twins could dodge
   And twist, with Rupert after—
Here, there, and everywhere they ran,
   With no thought of disaster

Next instant came a shout from Bill.
   "Look, look!" he cried, "poor Reg—
The cliff—he's gone—I saw him fall!
   He's gone right over the edge."

"What shall we do?" they, frightened, cried.
   Said Rupert: "We must try
To get him." Running to the edge,
   He heard a feeble cry.

Rupert climbed down in anxious haste
  To a ledge of rock below,
And there he stood. Oh dear! He found
  No further could he go.

  "Come back, come back!" Bill Badger cried,
    "Or you will fall down too."
So, sadly, Rupert scrambled back,
  It was all that he could do.

    "Bill, we must run to find some help
      As quickly as we can,"
    Said Rupert, "while we leave Rex here."
      Away the two then ran

Along the path that skirted the cliff.
  They called with frantic shouts:
"Help! Help!" and saw two boys ahead.
  Said Bill, "Here come two Scouts."

They ran up to the Scouts and cried,
  "Help, help! Please help us, do!
Our friend has fallen over the cliff,
  We tried to reach him too,

"But it was so steep." Said one Boy Scout,
  "Come on, Jack, let us run
And see what's happened; then we'll know
  If something can be done."

The Scouts ran quickly to the spot
  With Bill and Little Bear,
And cautiously looked over the cliff,
  But nothing could see there,

Or hear a sound—save Rex's sobs,
  And the beat of waves below.
"To get some rope," said one Boy Scout,
  "Ted, you must straightaway go."

Ted was not gone long before
    He came running back with rope
He'd borrowed from a nearby farm;
    "It's long enough, I hope,

"To reach him," he cried. The other Scout
    Got ready to descend
The steep cliff face. Ah! how they hoped
    He'd save their little friend.

The Scout climbed down the rope, and soon
    He saw poor little Reg
Lying senseless where he'd fallen
    Upon a narrow ledge

Halfway down the cliff. At once he found
    Reg had fainted with the pain
Of a broken arm. He picked him up
    And shouted back again

To those above he was coming up;
   Then carrying with care
Poor Reg, he soon climbed to the top,
   And brought him to safety there.

All anxiously the little friends gathered
   Round. "Oh," Rupert said,
"How is he?" Glad indeed they were
   To see he was not dead.

At once First Aid the Boy Scouts gave
   To his broken arm, and when
Poor Reg felt better, carefully they
   Lifted him up, and then

Said: "To a doctor he must go
   At once, without delay.
We'll take him to the village where
   One lives, now straightaway.

The little friends had told the Scouts
   They must let his Mummy know
What had happened. "Yes," they had replied,
   "At once to her you go."

So off ran Little Bear and Bill,
　And when they came in sight
Of Mrs. Bunny and Bill's Mum,
　They gave them such a fright.

"Reg has fallen down the cliff,"
　They called, "and broken his arm."
"What!" cried the mothers, jumping up,
　In a state of great alarm.

At once poor Mrs. Bunny ran to where
　Her quick eye spied
The Scouts approaching, one of whom
　Was carrying Reg. She cried:

"Oh, my poor child! What have you done?
　Thankful am I indeed
You were not killed; a doctor now
　Is our most urgent need.

"Does one live close?" she asked the Scouts.
　The boys replied: "We know
Of one in the village near at hand,
　It's not very far to go."

Reg was taken to a doctor,
　Where his broken arm was set.
When that was done his mother said:
　"Some tea now we must get."

She asked the Scouts to join them too,
　And not far from the sea,
In a cottage garden there they had
　A jolly country tea.

Soon came the time they must return,
    And as poor Reg was tired,
For painful was his broken arm,
    A motor-car was hired

To take them back to Winkle Bay.
    Quite sad were they to part
From the kind Boy Scouts, who'd helped them so.
    It was with grateful heart

That Mrs. Bunny thanked them both
    For all that they had done,
While Rupert waved with all his might
    Till out of sight they'd gone.

Next morning was fine. But poor Reg,
    Of course, had to stay in bed,
While the others took their morning walk
    And bathe. Bill's Mummy said,

"We must buy Reg a picture book
    To amuse him, poor little lad."
So at a stationer's shop they bought
    The nicest to be had.

6

Next day, as they walked on the beach,
   A boatman to them cried:
"Now, madam, a fine day for a row."
   "No, thanks," Bill's Mum replied.

For she did not like the sea at all,
   Because it made her ill.
"Wouldn't the young boys like to fish?"
   The man asked. "Oh!" cried Bill,

"Mummy, do let us! Please say yes!
   Just for an hour or so."
When she saw their eager, wistful looks,
   She said, "Yes, you may go."

How glad they were to be allowed
   To go out to sea and fish,
With the boatman's tackle, all supplied,
   Nothing better could they wish.

And Rupert bought some postcards, too,
   To send to Mummy Bear,
While Bill looked out some comic cards
   To send his friends from there.

Some distance out he rowed, then stopped,
And prepared for each some bait,
They lowered down their lines, and then
Eagerly they did wait.

When came the time their hour was up,
They'd caught about a score
Of whiting, mackerel and plaice.
They were rowed back to the shore.

Where Mrs. Badger waited for them.
"Oh, look!" they cried with glee,
"We've caught a lovely lot of fish.
Won't they be nice for tea?"

"Why yes," she said, "and now I think
It would be right to share
Your catch, and give some to poor Reg,
As he could not be there."

Next morning, walking by the sea,
Bill's mother said: "Now you
Can go and play. I'm going to knit.
Keep out of mischief, do."

So the little friends just wandered round.
It came into Bill's mind
That among the cliffs a smugglers' cave
With luck perhaps they'd find.

Bill, full of mischief, gave a jump,
    Then another—one, two, three,
Upon the springboard, which, of course,
    Threw poor Rex in the sea.

"Ha! Ha!" how Bill and Rupert laughed,
    When he came up again,
Spluttering, gasping for his breath;
    Soon to Little Bear it was plain,

That Rex would drown if they weren't quick,
    He saw he couldn't swim,
At least not much. "I say," he called.
    "We must go and rescue him."

They came to a rocky pool and stopped;
    They saw a springboard there.
Rex ventured on; without a word,
    Bill winked at Little Bear.

"I say," said Rex, as he gazed down
    Into the waters cool,
"I bet you chaps, though you can swim,
    Wouldn't dive into this pool."

Rupert plunged in and pulled Rex out,
  Screaming with all his might.
This brought Bill's Mummy running up,
  She was in such a fright.

"What's happened now?" she called to them,
  She helped them both to land;
"Where's Bill? Oh, you are tiresome boys,
  I cannot understand

"Why into mischief you must get.
  Now home you'll go," she cried;
"And straight to bed, and there you'll stay
  Until your clothes are dried."

* * *

So passed the days till came the time
  Their holiday had to end,
And they return. Now Rupert had
  Some money still to spend.

He saved it up because he knew
   His Mummy very soon
Would have a birthday. At a stall
   On their last afternoon

He saw a pretty box, the price
   He found that he could pay,
So counting out his money there,
   He bought it straightaway.

Little Rupert was soon home again
   From his holiday by the sea,
Where he had had a jolly time,
   But very glad was he

To be back with his Mum and Dad:
   "Oh, Mummy, dear!" he cried,
"I've bought this for your birthday, look!"
   And quickly she untied

The parcel. When she saw the box
   She cried: "Why this will do
For my sewing things. Thank you, dear,
   Such a lovely present, too."

Then Rupert had a lot to tell
   Of all that they had done
On holiday at Winkle Bay,
   With all its thrills and fun.

RUPERT
and the
Wonderful Boots

A knock came at Mrs. Bear's front door.
  When she opened it stood there
A Cobbler. "Ma'am," asked he,
  "Have you boots that need repair?"

"No," she replied, "I haven't." Said he,
  "I'm sorry," and turned to go;
But Rupert, who came up, said:
  "There's Dad's boots, Mum, you know."

"I'd quite forgotten those," she said.
  "I'll get them in a minute."
On his back the Cobbler had a sack.
  Rupert wondered what was in it.

Back with the boots came Mrs. Bear.
  "Now, mind you mend them well
And quickly," said she. "Ma'am," he said,
  "From new ones you won't tell

"These when I've finished. But have you
 A chair or stool to lend
That I may sit down here outside
 At once these boots to mend?"

Mum fetched a stool. The Cobbler sat
 And busily began
To mend the boots while Rupert watched
 That strange mysterious man.

Rupert thought he looked as though he'd stepped
 From a book of Fairy Tales,
In his funny hat and those strange clothes,
 As he hammered in the nails.

"Do you like mending boots?" he asked.
 Said the man: "Some boots I do;
I have a pair there in my sack
 Which I will show to you."

The Cobbler took out from his sack
　　What looked an ordinary pair
Of boots, and held them up with pride
　　To show to Little Bear.

"What do you think those are?" he said.
　　"A Wizard's boots, and he
Will trust none other in this world
　　To mend those boots but me."

"Oh," Rupert said with wondering eyes,
　　"Yes," the man said, "with these
He flies all over the countryside
　　And covers miles with ease.

"They're full of springs and tricky things;
　　Yet I've mended them all right:
But he'll give me aches and pains galore
　　If they're not back tonight."

Said the Cobbler, putting down the boots:
    "With them I've seen him spring
Over hedges, haystacks; even a house—
    In fact, over anything."

Then Dad's boots mended, up he stood.
    Mum was busy there inside;
The Cobbler knocked. "They're finished, ma'am,"
    To Mrs. Bear he cried.

"Just bring them in; I'm busy now,"
    To him called Mrs. Bear.
Rupert pondered on the Wizard's boots
    Which the Cobbler had left there.

He thought: "I wonder if it's true—
    All that he said just now
About those boots? To me they don't
    Look different anyhow

"From many others." Looking round,
    He saw the Cobbler had gone
Inside the house: and then at once
    He quickly slipped one on,

And then the other, over his own.
    Though large and loose a fit,
They firmly clung. Thought he: "I'll try
    To jump a little bit."

No sooner were the boots upon
 His feet than he gave a hop,
As up and down he sprang with ease,
 He did not want to stop.

With every hop he further sprang.
 It seemed such lovely fun;
Little he knew how it would end—
 This game he'd just begun.

Out came the Cobbler from the house
 Counting the money, for
He'd just been paid. He saw at once
 The boots were there no more.

They'd gone! Where were they? Then he saw
 Young Rupert up ahead.
"Hey! Hey!" he called. "Stop, come back,"
 As after him he sped.

Rupert soon found he'd had enough
 Of the boots, but could not stop:
However much he tried they still
 Went on—hop, hop, hop, hop!

When he heard the Cobbler calling
 And come running in his wake,
He hoped he'd catch him up and so
 From him those boots would take.

"Catch me, catch me!" Rupert called:
  But the Cobbler tried in vain,
For the boots and Rupert jumped a fence—
  And off he sprang again.

Hopping over the field he went
  With the Cobbler on his track:
Poor Mrs. Bear had joined the chase
  After this young spring-heeled Jack.

Then a team of horses in his way
  Rupert saw—to his great dread,
He could not stop; but with a spring
  Leaped right over their heads.

Still on he went. With every hop
  Yet faster, Rupert flew;
Stacks and hedges, meadows wide—
  He'd passed before he knew.

At the end of one long bound again
   The anxious Little Bear
Started coming down among
   Some children playing there.

Alarmed, they saw him come. "Look out!"
   He heard the children cry,
"There's someone falling down
   Upon us from the sky."

The children scattered. Down he bumped;
   But up he sprang again,
Carried higher. How he longed
   To stop—but longed in vain.

On, on he went high in the air
   Till right ahead did see
A village in his line of flight,
   With houses, church and trees.

Next moment he was flying over
  The roofs, while down below
Some passers-by did see him
  And, wondering, watched him go.

"Look! Look!" one called, "no bird is that,
  Flying in the air."
A butcher's boy, with sharp, sharp eyes,
  Cried: "It's a little bear."

The boots then took him higher up:
  With vast speed he did fly,
While frightened birds called in alarm
  At this stranger in the sky.

Past lakes and mountains on he went,
  Now fearing that he never
Would manage to end his reckless flight,
  And so would fly for ever.

At last Rupert felt he was going down.
  Below him he could see
An open grassy meadow where
  Stood one old apple tree.

A landing place! "Oh," Rupert thought,
  "If I could only stay!
But up the boots will spring again
  And carry me away!"

Bump! Down he came beside the tree,
  It was the merest chance
As up he sprang he managed to
  Grasp hold of a strong branch.

And there he swung. He dared not drop,
   For well he knew the trick
The Wizard's boots would work again—
   So to the branch he'd stick.

It happened that he had been seen
   On landing from the skies
By a little girl who tended geese.
   She scarce could trust her eyes

To see a bear from nowhere fall.
   She came up cautiously,
And stared amazed at Rupert small
   Up in the apple tree.

"Oh, do," he said, "pull off my boots."
   She turned about to flee
It seemed so queer. What did it mean?
   "Oh, please," again said he.

She summoned all her courage up,
   And went up to the Bear.
"Why do you want them off?" she asked,
   "And why such large boots wear?"

"Oh, please, be quick, or I shall drop.
   Then I'll be off again,"
Said Rupert to her, "for my arms
   Can't stand this awful strain."

Puzzled still, she reached up then,
   And from his feet pulled she
The Wizard's boots. Down Rupert dropped
   Oh, how relieved was he!

He thanked the little girl. "These boots
   Have led me such a dance,"
Said he. "They've carried me for miles,
   Till I dropped here by chance.

"But where am I, and where is this?"
   The girl, who'd lost her fear,
Said: "It belongs to two old Dwarfs,
   My masters, who live near."

Rupert almost thought to leave
   The boots behind him there;
But still they might be useful—
   So he picked up the pair.

Said he: "I'm feeling tired,
   Hungry and thirsty, too."
Said she: "The Dwarfs are kind. I'm sure
   Some food they'll give to you."

They soon approached a farmyard, where
   Busy working round about
Were two strange-looking little men—
   One lean, the other stout.

Said the little girl to these two men:
   "Please sirs, this little bear
Was hanging in our apple tree.
   He fell down from the air."

"Oh!" said the Dwarfs—for such they were.
   The little girl told them
Of Rupert's hunger. "Give him food,
   And welcome," said the men.

The little girl brought Rupert food,
   And he sat down to eat.
The Dwarfs had noticed those strange boots,
   So big for Rupert's feet.

Said they: "Why did you carry these?"
    For coming to the farm
They'd noticed he'd one in his hand
    And one beneath his arm.

Then Rupert told about the boots—
    How they had brought him there.
"That's wonderful," the brothers said,
    Examining the pair

Inside and out. "And did you say
    That all those miles they've flown?"
"Yes," Rupert said. Then came the thought—
    Those boots they'd like to own.

The Dwarfs had told the little girl
    When Rupert's meal was done
To show him to the attic room
    To sleep till came the sun.

Rupert took care not to forget
   The boots, as up he rose.
He followed her as, candle in hand,
   To him the way she showed.

Soon as he'd gone the Dwarfs both planned
   How at the break of day
They'd go upstairs while still he slept
   And take those boots away.

Rupert woke to hear the birds
   Greeting the sun at dawn;
Wondered for a moment where he was,
   Then sat up with a yawn.

Then—hist!—what was that on the stairs?
   Surely a stealthy tread
Was drawing near! Rupert jumped;
   Sat listening in his bed.

Whispering voices he could hear:
   "If he makes any fuss,
Remember, brother, what to do!
   Then those boots belong to us."

Poor Rupert, trembling, jumped from bed,
  As quietly as he could,
Slipping on the boots just as the Dwarfs
  Opened the door of wood.

That he'd not left the Wizard's boots
  Downstairs he was glad indeed,
For though they'd played him tricks he hoped
  They'd serve him now in need.

Open further came the door.
  One glance cast Little Bear
At the window. Yes, it was large enough
  For him to spring through there.

Next instant in the thin Dwarf dashed
  To see Rupert give a bound
Out through the window. "Ha!" he cried,
  But was too late, he found.

The boots served Rupert well this time.
  Wild were the little men
At losing so those wondrous boots!
  Each blamed the other then.

Away went Rupert once again,
  While from the window there
The thin Dwarf shrieked his wrath and shook
  His fist at Little Bear.

Rupert was carried by the boots
  At their capricious whim
Over hill and dale. He wondered where
  The boots would next take him.

At length Rupert felt himself descend
  Just as he saw below
A castle with its towers and moat.
  Down, down the boots did go.

As down the Wizard's boots did fall,
  He clutched hard at a wall
To stop himself, and there he clung
  Afraid in the moat he'd fall.

From a window an old woman saw
  Him falling from the air;
Looking out, she thought: "What can that be?
  I'll see what's happened there."

The old woman hurried out to him,
  She said: "Oh, dear! Oh, dear!
You poor little thing! I'll help you up.
  However came you here?"

She'd only come there just in time;
  His hands were letting go;
If he lost his hold then she'd not save
  Him from the moat below.

"Now, trust yourself to me," she said,
  Pulling him to safety there
Over the parapet. Quite easily
  She lifted the Little Bear.

When she'd set Rupert gently down,
  "Do, please, pull off," said he,
"These boots, for if I move a step
  Away they'll carry me."

Amazed, she stared as Rupert told
  How those boots had carried him.
"I wish they'd take me home," he said,
  "But they go at their whim."

What plans were passing in her mind;
  To whom she went or where,
As with a kindly glance she left
  Him standing lonely there.

She stooped and pulled them from his feet.
  "Of these boots tell me more.
Come to my room nearby," said she.
  "I've not heard this before."

When they reached her room, "Wait here," she said.
  "I'll fetch you food and drink.
You must be tired; I'll come back soon."
  Little did Rupert think

She closed the door; he heard a key
  Turn sharp. He was locked in!
Where were the boots? He had not seen
  She'd left them not within.

Now that old dame was housekeeper
  To an Ogre fierce and grim
Who owned that castle—so she went
  Straight away to tell to him

Of Little Bear and the wondrous boots.
    Now, of him she went in fear.
Thought she: "It will please him if I tell
    The news of what's come here."

The Ogre sat in his big chair: ugly,
    Swarthy and fat was he.
The old dame first tapped at his door,
    Then entered timidly.

"I thought," said she, "it might please you,
    If I showed you this pair
Of wondrous boots I took just now
    From a curious Little Bear.

"He said that they had carried him
    Miles and miles high in the air."
"What?" growled the Ogre. "Bring him here!
    A fine tale, I do swear!"

The old dame returned with Rupert soon,
　　Who was frightened when he did see
That ugly Ogre sitting there.
　　"What's this?" he bawled, "tell me.

And pulled and tugged, and tugged and pulled;
　　But on it would not go—
Till—"Stop!" the Ogre roared in wrath,
　　"You're hurting my foot so.

"I don't believe the tale you've told
　　About what those boots can do.
But I'm going to try them on and see
　　If what you've said is true."

"Come," said the Ogre testily,
　　Thrusting out his foot.
The dame knew they were far too small,
　　As she picked up a boot,

"That's proof to me he spoke not truth.
　　For Magic boots would fit.
They're ordinary ones. I don't
　　Believe his tale one bit.

"Here, put them on yourself! I'll see
　　If what you say is true,"
The Ogre shouted. "If it's false
　　It will be the worse for you."

Just as Rupert picked up a boot
　　The Ogre at him dashed
　　The other; Rupert dodged in time
　　As on the floor it crashed.

Quickly Rupert put on the boots,
　　For his sharp eyes had spied
What they had overlooked; it was
　　A window at the side.

To the window Rupert ran;
　　Arrived, and with a spring,
Through that window he was gone,
　　Like a bird upon the wing.

He was off and free! He'd got away!
  The dame was rather glad;
But the Ogre, seeing him escape
  With fury was half mad.

The boots once more had him in charge.
  Through them he'd got away
From that dread Ogre: by their aid
  He was saved again that day.

But he was tired of flying wild;
  Wandering just where
The boots took him. "Oh, dear, for home,"
  Thought weary Little Bear.

At the end of one long bound he landed
  And up again did spring.
He gripped a signpost with both hands;
  Firmly to it did cling.

Rupert pulled and struggled up until
    On the signpost he did sit.
He tried to get those big boots off:
    But each was a close fit.

Very soon he heard the sound of hoofs,
    And saw a boy appear
Riding a horse from the nearby forge,
    "Hullo," cried the boy, "what's here?"

"Oh," said Rupert, "pull off these boots!"
    How the farmer's boy did stare.
"Well," he said, "that should be easy,
    When such big boots you wear."

So saying he gave each a tug
    And then off came each one.
"There," laughed the boy, "you see that job
    Very easily was done."

When the farmer's boy had ridden off
    Quickly the Little Bear
Climbed down the signpost and picked up
    The boots left lying there.

Thought he those boots he'd better keep,
    But still not put them on,
For then they'd take him off again
    On another mad-cap run.

So on he walked until he saw
 A forest loom ahead.
"Oh, for a place where I could rest!
 I am so tired!" he said.

In a quiet glade, beneath an oak,
 There in the forest deep
Rupert lay down; tired as he was
 He soon fell fast asleep.

Now a Robber prowling through the wood
 Spied Rupert. Drawing near,
From tree to tree—"Ho! Ho!" thought he,
 "Whatever have we here?"

With stealthy, silent tread he moved
Carefully on his toes
And making not the slightest sound,
To Rupert he did go.

The Robber, when he saw the boots
By the sleeping Little Bear,
Thought: "Ha! The very things I want,
I do need a new pair."

That evil Robber snatched both boots,
Of course he did not know
That they were not the usual kind,
But were Magic boots, as you know.

Up Rupert jumped. How scared was he
To see that rascal there
Clutching the boots. "Give them to me.
Do, please!" cried Little Bear.

"Be off," the Robber gruffly said,
"Or I'll make an end of you!
These boots are mine; I've got them now,
And mean to keep them too."

The Robber's manner suddenly changed;
   Rupert looked round and saw
A little girl of whom the thief
   Stood certainly in awe.

In haughty tones she spoke to him:
   "I saw what passed. Beware,
Or you'll be strung from a stout oak tree
   If you harm that Little Bear."

The Robber cringed. He spoke not to
   The little girl. Now she
Was daughter of the Robber Chief:
   All powerful was he.

"As for those boots, keep them yourself"—
   Proudly she tossed her head—
"But this Little Bear he shall be mine.
   I'll take him home," she said.

"You come with me," said the little girl,
   "My playmate and pet to be."
She seized his hand to pull him on,
   But quickly drew back he.

"Come," she called to the Robber there,
   "Take hold of his other hand.
He cannot get away from us;
   He soon will understand."

So in their power he was led
   Deep into the forest where
What would happen next to him
   Rupert wondered in despair.

Through twisting paths and secret ways
   That none but the Robbers knew
Rupert was taken, till at length
   A rock came into view.

Before its rocky face they stopped.
   The Robber pulled away
A small stone slab, which Robert saw
   An opening did display.

Not large enough it looked indeed
   For a man to crawl inside.
"We'll go in there," said the little girl.
   "No! No!" poor Rupert cried.

If only he could get away;
    But his hands were held so tight!
He saw the boots, but there was no chance
    To use their Magic Flight.

Inside the secret hole they crawled,
    On hands and knees did go—
First the girl, then Rupert next,
    With the Robber last, and so

Some way they crept. Pitch dark it was.
    At length they stood upright
And climbed some steps. On, on they went;
    It was still as dark as night.

At a turning in the rock-hewn stairs
    A light there pierced the gloom,
Showing in the cave—for such it was—
    That the stairs led to a room.

To the Robbers' stronghold they had come:
    It was their secret lair.
All brightly lit, the light at first
    Dazzled the Little Bear.

Then he saw rough men seated round
   A table. Towards one ran
The little girl. "Look, Father, look,"
   She called out to the man.

He was the Robber Chief. Beside him sat
   His old mother, harsh and grim;
And when she saw the Little Bear
   Evil smiles she cast at him.

"Come," said the little girl, "sit down;
   We'll eat—just me and you,"
And from a steaming cauldron took
   For each some savoury stew.

As Rupert was eating from his bowl
   The woman came. Said she,
With an Ogress leer: "A tasty bite
   That Bear will make for me."

"No, Granny! He belongs to me!
   Not a finger shall be laid
On him. Or I'll tell my father.
   He's mine!" the little girl said.

The old dame scowled at her, but dared
   Not answer in reply
To the Chieftain's daughter, for she knew
   In his favour she was high.

When they'd had their meal the little girl
　　Said: "To bed now, Little Bear."
Rupert saw no bed, but some hay spread
　　And a blanket lying there.

She flung herself dressed as she was
　　Down there and then to sleep:
But with caution she on Rupert's hand
　　A firm hold yet did keep.

Soon she was fast in slumber bound,
　　But Rupert still could hear
The men carousing noisily:
　　He sat up there in fear.

The tears stole down his cheeks. He cried.
   He was in such misery!
"No one," he thought, "can find me here.
   What will become of me?"

Rupert's sobs woke up the little girl.
   "What's the matter now?" she cried.
He turned to her: "Oh, please help me!"
   She sat up in surprise.

He told her of the wondrous boots.
   Pleaded he: "If I could get
Those boots, and you would let me go,
   I might get back home yet."

All was quiet now but for the snores
  Of the Robbers, now asleep.
They lay about the floor: their dog
  Alone his guard did keep.

Up jumped the little girl. She said:
  "You come along with me;
You'll have those boots, poor Little Bear,
  And I will set you free."

She took his hand to seek for them
  Among the Robbers there
When the dog on guard up fiercely sprang
  Towards the Little Bear.

"Be quiet!" she said. "Lie down." At once
  The dog, growling, obeyed;
It was well this did not rouse the men
  Among whom their way they made.

They found the Robber they did seek.
  Beside him where he slept
Lay one boot, while beneath his arm
  The other was. Up crept

The little girl, while Rupert watched
  To see how cleverly
That boot from underneath his arm,
  Not waking him, pulled she.

Then she picked up the other one,
  And quickly on tiptoe
Through sleeping men they made their way
  And from the cavern did go.

Down the steps from the cavern room
  She led him till once more
They came to the secret opening through
  Which they had crawled before.

He was outside and free. "But wait,"
  She said, "I'll be a minute."
Soon she came back. "Take this. You'll see
  Some food I've put within it.

"And here's a stick. Go straight along
    The secret track," said she,
"Where here and there a white stone shows,
    Till of the forest you're free.

"Once there, perhaps someone you'll meet
    Who maybe to you can tell
The way your home lies. So goodbye."
    She waved to him farewell.

Through the forest he trudged on
    Where the white stones lay;
As the little girl had told, they showed
    The Robbers' Secret Way.

At length he reached the forest's edge
    Where trees did thinly grow—
Glad to leave the woods behind
    For the sunlit vale below.

When Rupert wandered on and left
   The forest well behind
He grew so hungry he sat down
   To see what food he'd find.

In the bundle which the little girl
   Had given him there were
Two meat pies, with some bread and cheese.
   Then a voice came: "Can you spare

   "A little for a poor old soul?"
      Rupert looked up in surprise
   To see an old woman. "Yes," he said,
      Giving her one of his pies.

The woman thanked him for the pie
   Which she ate beside him there.
Then, pointing to the boots, she said:
   "How came you by that pair?

"I know those boots." Then Rupert told
How they'd carried him from home;
Now he was lost; nor did he dare
Put them on, or off he'd roam.

The dame was a Fairy in disguise.
She knew their secret well.
Said she: "Those boots shall carry you
To any place I tell."

Said she to Rupert: "Now, put on
Those boots." "Oh, no," said he,
"For they'll carry me away again."
Said she: "Just trust to me.

"I'll help you on with them. Now, boots,"
He heard the old dame tell,
"Take Little Bear to the Cobbler who
Has mended you so well.

"Then he shall to the Wizard go
And straight away restore
You to your Master." Then (to Rupert):
"You'll soon be home once more."

The dame stood up. "Come, boots," she said,
"This time you'll homeward fly!"
Then facing Rupert straight for home,
"Be off," she called, "goodbye."

Up with a bound the boots took him
Almost before he knew,
Over hill and dale, woodland and vale,
Like a bird on the wing he flew.

At length he felt the boots descend,
  And there to his surprise
He saw the Cobbler, arms outstretched
  To catch him. "Ah!" he cried,

"At last I've got you, you Young Bear.
  It is a lucky chance
That I was here. I guess those boots
  Led you a pretty dance.

When he'd been carried miles and miles
  Landmarks came into view,
Farm and cottage, orchards, fields
  And places that he knew.

"You'll come with me now straight away
  To the Wizard. Oh, the pain
He's giving me for punishment
  Till he gets those boots again."

To the Wizard's house the Cobbler went
    Telling Rupert to wait outside;
Which, indeed, he much preferred to do.
    "Here they are," the Cobbler cried,

Holding a boot in either hand.
    "I've brought them back all right.
Look for yourself, and, master, please
    Don't punish me tonight."

"Humph!" said the Wizard, looking round,
    Busy with potions there;
"If this happens again your punishment
    Will come to stay. Beware!"

Relieved the boots were now safe home,
    The Cobbler took Rupert where
He knew his mother, anxious, waited
    For news of Little Bear.

Soon the Cottage they approached,
    Rupert ran on before;
But his mother had already seen,
    And come out from the door.

"Mummy! Mummy! I'm back!" he cried.
    Happy that he was found,
She clasped him in her arms, so glad
    That he was safe and sound.

RUPERT

and the
Twin's Birthday Cake

"I say," said Bill to Little Bear,
    When unexpectedly they met;
"Have you had an invitation to
    The Birthday Party yet?"

"What Birthday Party?" Rupert asked.
    "Reggie and Rex, you know.
They've just asked me," Bill Badger said,
    "Of course, you too will go."

Just at that time Reggie and Rex
    To Rupert's house were bound
To invite him to their party.
    Mrs. Bear at home they found.

"Rupert's out, my dears," his Mummy said.
    "Oh, please," the Twins replied,
"May he come to our party? It's on Tuesday."
    Then each vied

In telling her about their cake
Ordered from Mr. Dough.
Mummy, much amused, said Rupert
Could to their party go.

The Twins hurried off, they'd much to do,
And other friends to invite
To their Birthday Party. Down the road
Little Bear came into sight.

"Rupert!" both cried, "your Mum says you can
Come to our party!" Then
They told of their cake to be on show
Next day at the baker's at ten.

So next morning Rupert and Bill
Found their way to the shop,
To see Reggie and Rex's Birthday Cake.
There to admire it they stopped.

A gorgeous cake it was to see,
Coated in sugar so white,
Decked with candied fruits, pink letters too,
It was a pretty sight.

As they passed on, next came along
   Hubert and Wally, that pair,
Who were always out to bully and tease
   Bill Badger and Little Bear.

"Coo," cried Wally Wolf. "Look at that cake."
   Next moment he did see
The Twins' names written underneath;
   "Why, it's for them," cried he.

"A Birthday Cake! and we're not asked
   To tea with them that day.
I'd like to spoil their party, Bert,
   If we could find some way."

That afternoon it happened that
   A lucky chance they found;
For Mr. Dough's baker boy
   They saw upon his round.

They hoped that he might have the cake
  Within his barrow there,
And as he went to leave some bread,
  To peep in they prepared.

They waited till the baker's boy
  Had gone to leave some bread,
And when he'd disappeared from sight,
  Hubert and Wally sped

Towards his barrow; Hubert watched
  While Wally looked inside;
"We are in luck, the cake is here!"
  Triumphantly he cried.

Next instant Wally seized the cake,
  And he and Hubert ran
Away with it. They left the road
  Before the chase began

And climbed a stile to cross some fields;
  Their object was to find
A safe and secret hiding-place
  And leave the cake behind.

They little knew they had been seen
  For, just there by the stile,
Was Willie Hedgehog hunting snails,
  Who'd watched them all the while.

Within a wood, they hunted round,
    Until at length did see
The very place to hide the cake
    Within a hollow tree.

In haste the wily Wally Wolf
    Pushed the cake inside,
And covered it with leaves and moss,
    So nothing could be spied.

Well pleased, the two then walked away,
    Chuckling at what they'd done.
To spoil Rex and Reggie's birthday so,
    They thought the greatest fun.

Now Wally and Hubert had been seen
    By a little Squirrel there,
Who guessed on mischief they were bent,
    They were a well-known pair.

So off he scampered in hot haste,
  And glad was he to see
Rupert and Bill. He quickly told
  About the hollow tree.

And the mystery parcel there within.
  "What can it be?" said they.
"You come with me," the Squirrel said,
  "I can show you the way."

The two friends followed where he led
  Till he stopped before a tree,
And, pointing, said: "You'll find it there,
  It's hidden carefully."

Rupert pulled aside the moss and leaves,
  Then how he stared, surprised
To see a large white parcel there
  Addressed to the Twins. He cried:

"It's from Mr. Dough, and, Bill, I'm sure
  It's the Birthday Cake, no doubt,"
And with that from its hiding-place
  He quickly pulled it out.

Glad were they to have foiled the trick
  Played by that wily pair,
And to take the cake back to the Twins
  They there and then prepared.

The cake between them, off they walked;
  When by chance there came that way,
Across the fields the guilty pair;
  "Hi, Hubert! Look, I say!"

Said Wally Wolf, "There's Rupert Bear,
  And they have found the cake.
What's to be done? I know," he said,
  "For the baker's shop we'll make."

Wally and Hubert hurried off,
  And met the baker's boy,
For it suited their purpose better still
  To tell with gleeful joy

That Rupert and Bill had got the cake;
    The boy looked in to see
If it was in his barrow, found it gone,
    Then shouted excitedly:

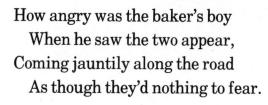

        "Where did you see them?" They replied,
            "Along the road down there."
        At once the baker's boy ran off
            To catch Bill and Little Bear.

        How angry was the baker's boy
            When he saw the two appear,
        Coming jauntily along the road
            As though they'd nothing to fear.

        "How dare you steal that cake?" he yelled,
            "I know you took it, so,
        You give it back to me at once,
            Or to the police I'll go."

He snatched the cake away from them,
    And gripping Rupert's arm,
"I'll tell your Dad," he said, while Bill,
    In anger and alarm,

Cried out: "We didn't steal the cake,
    We found it in a tree."
"A likely tale," then sneered the boy,
    "You come along with me

"And tell my master that," and he began
    To bully them and shout,
Till a Policeman, coming down the road, said:
    "What's this all about?"

The baker's boy soon told his tale,
    That they did steal the cake.
"We didn't!" Bill and Rupert sobbed;
    "He's made a great mistake.

"We found it in a tree," they said.
    The Policeman said: "We'll see.
We'll soon find out about this, so
    You come along with me."

Now Willie Hedgehog, hunting snails,
    Had overheard again
And seen what happened, and to him
    The truth was very plain.

Rupert and Bill were innocent
    The culprits, well he knew,
Were Hubert Hippo, Wally Wolf.
    Now what could Willie do?

He ambled off straight for the wood,
    And meeting Squirrel there,
He told him what had happened to
    Poor Bill and Little Bear.

Indignant at injustice done
     To Rupert, they did vote
The very best thing they could do
     Was to tell the Wise Old Goat.

"He'll know what to do," they both agreed
     And quickly they repaired
To the Wise Goat's house—he was at home
     And reading in his chair.

The Wise Goat listened to their tale,
     Then up he quietly rose,
And asked them to accompany him,
     "To Rupert's help we go."

The Wise Goat with the witnesses
     Went first to Mr. Dough,
And told of Bill and Rupert's plight,
     Which to the baker's boy they owed.

"Ridiculous!" said Mr. Dough,
     "Of course they wouldn't take
The Twins' own Birthday Cake—
     It's clear there's a mistake."

To Mrs. Bunny next they went,
     Who, told they had been charged
Said, "Stuff and nonsense! We must see
     At once they're set at large."

To the Police they hurried then,
     Each witness told his tale.
The charge being false, Rupert and Bill
     Were soon let out of gaol.

How glad indeed was everyone
　　As they walked side by side
For home—Willie sat on Rupert's arm,
　　While Squirrel had a ride

On Wise Goat's shoulder; lucky it was
　　They'd seen those culprits bold,
Hubert and Wally, at their tricks,
　　And so the truth was told

To the Police. Rupert and Bill,
　　Now proved innocent,
Were delighted all had ended well, as
　　Homeward then they went.

So the Party soon took place
　　And all the friends were there,
Except, as you will guess, of course,
　　That wily, wicked pair,

Hubert and Wally, who had tried
　　Their best to spoil the fun
By stealing Rex and Reggie's cake,
　　They weren't missed by anyone.

The Wise Old Goat, he cut the cake
　　When the time came for tea;
Each had a share, so ended then
　　The Party happily.